USBORNE KEY

Practice Pad
Times Tables

Written by Sam Smith

Illustrated by Maddie Frost

Designed by Laura Hammonds,
Winsome d'Abreu and
Carly Davies

Series Editor: Felicity Brooks

$$3 \times 2 = 6$$

Once you've completed an activity sheet from this pad,
you can check it using the answer pages at the back.

Here are the animals you'll meet as you work through the activities.

Coco the raccoon

Bun the rabbit

You can tear off the sheets to take out with you for practice wherever you are.

Olly the owl

Foxy the fox

Mo the mouse

Moley the mole

Squilly the squirrel

Hug the bear

Stripe the badger

Spike the hedgehog

2 more

Count the berries in each group below, then
draw 2 more. Write the numbers in the boxes.

How many berries above?	Add	2 more berries.	How many berries now?

2 + 2 = 4

Mmm, those
berries look
delicious!

How many berries above?	Add	2 more berries.	How many berries now?

4 + 2 =

2 more

Count the shells in each group below, then
draw 2 more. Write the numbers in the boxes.

| How many shells above? | Add | 2 more shells. | How many shells now? |

 + **2** **=**

| How many shells above? | Add | 2 more shells. | How many shells now? |

 + **2** **=**

2 more

Count the balls in each group below, then
draw 2 more. Write the numbers in the boxes.

How many balls above?	Add	2 more balls.	How many balls now?
10	+	2 =	12

How many balls above?	Add	2 more balls.	How many balls now?
12	+	2 =	14

2 more

Count the berries in each group below, then
draw 2 more. Write the numbers in the boxes.

How many
berries above?   Add

2 more
berries.

How many
berries now?

 +   **2**   **=**

How many
berries above?   Add

2 more
berries.

How many
berries now?

16   **+**   **2**   **=**   18

Sock twos

Help Spike count up the socks in twos. Follow the arrows, and write the new total under each group.

Honeycomb

Find a route across the honeycomb. The next cell's number must always be 2 more than the number of the cell you are on.

Start

6 9

3 4 7 15 18

1 2 5 8 10 13 11

7 4 6 11 12 19

8 9 5 7 14 17 8

14 12 8 13 16 15

16 17 19 15 14 18 19

18 20 16 18 20

17 19

Finish

Sequences

Fill in the missing numbers in these sequences so that each number is 2 more than the one before.

2   4   6   8

12   14   16   18

4   6   8   10

8   10   12   14

Sequences

Write the missing numbers in these sequences so
that each number is 2 more than the one before.

6 8 10 12

10 12 14 16

4 6 8 10

14 16 18 20

Adding in twos

For each calculation, count up the socks in twos, then write the total number of socks in the empty box.

+ = 4

What a lot of socks!

+ + = 12

+ + + = 12

+ + + + = 22

Adding in twos

For each calculation, draw the final two socks, then write the total number of socks in the empty box.

$2 + 2 + 2 + 2 + 2 = 10$

$2 + 2 + 2 = $

That's a big pen, Mo!

$2 + 2 = 4$

$2 + 2 + 2 + 2 = $

Adding in twos

Help Moley add up these numbers,
and write the totals in the boxes.

$2 + 2 + 2 = 6$

Hold it steady,
Stripe!

$2 + 2 + 2 + 2 + 2 = \boxed{}$

$2 + 2 + 2 + 2 + 2 + 2 = \boxed{}$

$2 + 2 + 2 + 2 + 2 + 2 + 2 = \boxed{}$

2 4 6 8 10 12 14 16 18 20

Groups of 2

Spike and his friend are taking a nature walk.
Trace over the numbers in the boxes at
the bottom to finish the sentence.

Groups of 2

A pair of friends have joined the hedgehogs'
walk. Write the numbers in the boxes at
the bottom to finish the sentence.

2 groups of 2 friends = ☐ friends altogether

2 4 6 8 10 12 14 16 18 20

Groups of 2

A pair of moles have joined the hedgehogs and raccoons on their walk. Write the numbers in the boxes at the bottom to finish the sentence.

Are we nearly there?

3 groups of 2 friends = [ ] friends altogether

2 4 6 8 10 12 14 16 18 20

Groups of 2

Moley has spotted some butterflies in groups of 2.
Circle each group, then write the numbers in the
boxes at the bottom to finish the sentence.

4 groups of 2 butterflies = [ ] butterflies altogether

2   4   6   8   10   12   14   16   18   20

Groups of 2

Moley is watching these groups of 2 butterflies.
Circle each group, then write the numbers in the
boxes at the bottom to finish the sentence.

5 groups of 2 butterflies = ☐ butterflies altogether

2 4 6 8 10 12 14 16 18 20

Groups of 2

Hug has spotted some dragonflies flying in groups of 2. Circle each group, then write the numbers in the boxes at the bottom to finish the sentence.

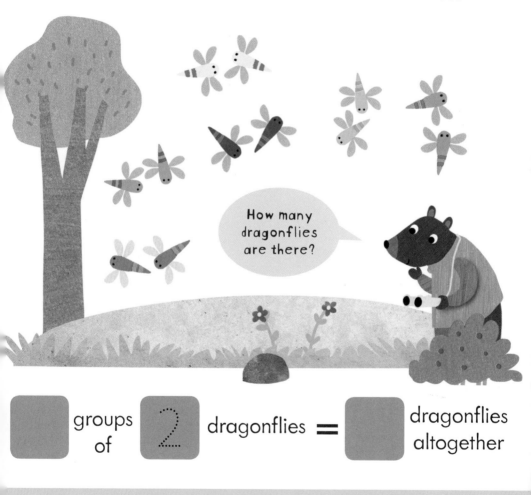

How many dragonflies are there?

[ ] groups of 2 dragonflies = [ ] dragonflies altogether

2 4 6 8 10 12 14 16 18 20

Groups of 2

Hug is watching these groups of 2 dragonflies. Circle each group, then write the numbers in the boxes at the bottom to finish the sentence.

☐ groups of 2 dragonflies = ☐ dragonflies altogether

2 4 6 8 10 12 14 16 18 20

Groups of 2

Coco has spotted some birds in groups of 2.
Circle each group, then write the numbers in
the boxes at the bottom to finish the sentence.

How many
birds are
there?

☐ groups
of 2 birds = ☐ birds
altogether

2 4 6 8 10 12 14 16 18 20

Groups of 2

Coco is watching these groups of 2 birds.
Circle each group, then write the numbers in
the boxes at the bottom to finish the sentence.

Can you help me count all the birds?

 groups of birds = birds altogether

2 4 6 8 10 12 14 16 18 20

Groups of 2

Foxy has spotted some bees in groups of 2.
Circle each group, then write the numbers in
the boxes at the bottom to finish the sentence.

How many bees are there?

[ ] groups of 2 bees = [ ] bees altogether

2 4 6 8 10 12 14 16 18 20

Equal groups

Describe these groups in two different ways.
Write in the empty boxes how many groups there
are, and how many snails there are altogether.

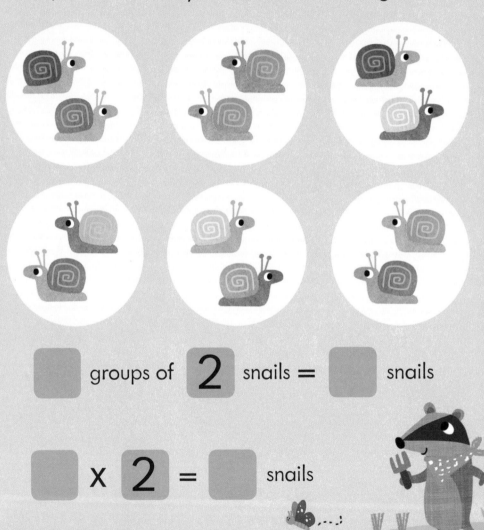

☐ groups of **2** snails = ☐ snails

☐ x **2** = ☐ snails

Equal groups

Describe these groups in two different ways.
Write in the empty boxes how many groups there
are, and how many leaves there are altogether.

groups of **2** leaves = leaves

☐ x **2** = ☐ leaves

Equal groups

Describe these groups in two different ways.
Write in the empty boxes how many groups there
are, and how many snakes there are altogether.

 groups of **2** snakes = [ ] snakes

[ ] x **2** = [ ] snakes

Equal groups

Describe this group in two different ways.
Write in the empty boxes how many groups there
are, and how many trees there are altogether.

☐ group of **2** trees = ☐ trees

☐ x **2** = ☐ trees

Equal groups

Describe these groups in two different ways.
Write in the empty boxes how many groups there
are, and how many clouds there are altogether.

groups of **2** clouds = clouds

× **2** = clouds

Equal groups

Describe these groups in two different ways.
Write in the empty boxes how many groups there
are, and how many kites there are altogether.

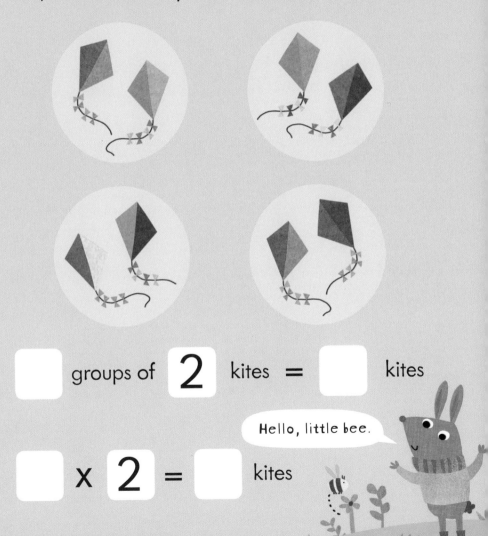

☐ groups of **2** kites = ☐ kites

Hello, little bee.

☐ x **2** = ☐ kites

Equal groups

Describe these groups in two different ways.
Write in the empty boxes how many groups there
are, and how many flowers there are altogether.

[ ] groups of **2** flowers = [ ] flowers

[ ] x **2** = [ ] flowers

Equal groups

Describe these groups in two different ways.
Write in the empty boxes how many groups there
are, and how many shells there are altogether.

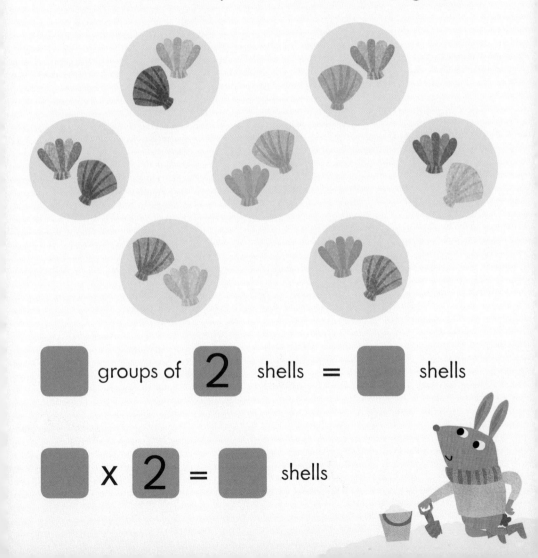

☐ groups of **2** shells = ☐ shells

☐ x **2** = ☐ shells

Equal groups

Describe these groups in two different ways.
Write in the empty boxes how many groups there
are, and how many fish there are altogether.

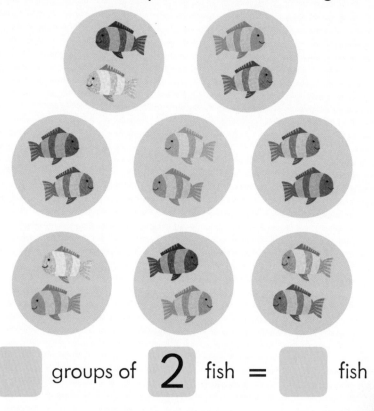

[ ] groups of **2** fish = [ ] fish

[ ] x **2** = [ ] fish

Equal groups

Describe these groups in two different ways.
Write in the empty boxes how many groups there
are, and how many stars there are altogether.

☐ groups of **2** stars = ☐ stars

☐ x **2** = ☐ stars

Calculation pairs

Stripe and Squilly have been collecting acorns. Fill in the numbers in the calculations below to see how many acorns they each have, and to see if Squilly is right.

I think we both have the same number of acorns, Stripe!

Stripe's calculation:

2   x   9   =

Squilly's calculation:

9   x   2   =

Calculation pairs

Fill in the blanks to complete two different calculations for each group of toys. One has been done for you.

$$10 \times 2 = 20$$
$$2 \times 10 = 20$$

...... $\times 2$ = ...

...... $\times 3$ = ...

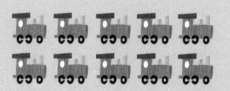

$5 \times$ ...... = ...

$2 \times$ ...... = ...

...... $\times$ ...... = ...

...... $\times$ ...... = ...

Calculation pairs

Fill in the blanks to complete two different calculations
for each group of animals. One has been done for you.

$4 \times 2 = 8$

$2 \times 4 = 8$

...... $\times 2 = $ ......

$2 \times $ ...... $= $ ......

$7 \times $ ...... $= $ ......

$2 \times $ ...... $= $ ......

$9 \times $ ...... $= $ ......

$2 \times $ ...... $= $ ......

2 times table

Trace over the dotted numbers and fill in the empty boxes to finish these calculations in the 2 times table.

1 x 2 = ☐　　6 x 2 = ☐

2 x 2 = ☐　　7 x 2 = ☐

3 x 2 = ☐　　8 x 2 = ☐

4 x 2 = ☐　　9 x 2 = ☐

5 x 2 = ☐　　10 x 2 = ☐

2 times table

Trace over the dotted numbers and fill in the empty boxes to finish these calculations in the 2 times table.

2 x 1 = ☐   2 x 6 = ☐

2 x 2 = ☐   2 x 7 = ☐

2 x 3 = ☐   2 x 8 = ☐

2 x 4 = ☐   2 x 9 = ☐

2 x 5 = ☐   2 x 10 = ☐

Calculation match-up

Help Bun finish these calculations. Draw a
line to match each one to its answer.
One has been done for you.

8 x 2

18

9 x 2

2 x 5

4

10

16

8

2 x 6

7 x 2

2 x 2

12

14

2 x 4

How many twos?

Finish these calculations for Stripe and Squilly. To help, you could draw around groups of 2 blossoms until they are all in groups, then count the groups.

☐ x 2 = 10

☐ x 2 = 14

How many twos?

Complete these calculations for Stripe and Squilly.
To help, you could draw around groups of 2 cherries
until they are all in groups, then count the groups.

□ x 2 = 8

□ x 2 = 16

How many twos?

Finish these calculations for Stripe and Squilly.
To help, you could draw around groups of 2 apples
until they are all in groups, then count the groups.

☐ x 2 = 12

☐ x 2 = 2

How many twos?

Complete these calculations for Stripe and Squilly.
To help, you could draw around groups of 2 acorns
until they are all in groups, then count the groups.

☐ x 2 = 6

☐ x 2 = 18

How many twos?

Finish these calculations for Stripe and Squilly.
To help, you could draw around groups of 2 plums
until they are all in groups, then count the groups.

☐ x 2 = 4

☐ x 2 = 20

Missing numbers

Write the missing numbers in the boxes to finish these calculations from the 2 times table.

$\boxed{} \times 2 = 2$

$2 \times \boxed{} = 8$

$9 \times 2 = \boxed{}$

$2 \times \boxed{} = 14$

$\boxed{} \times 2 = 4$

$2 \times 5 = \boxed{}$

Missing numbers

Fill in the missing numbers in the boxes to finish these calculations from the 2 times table.

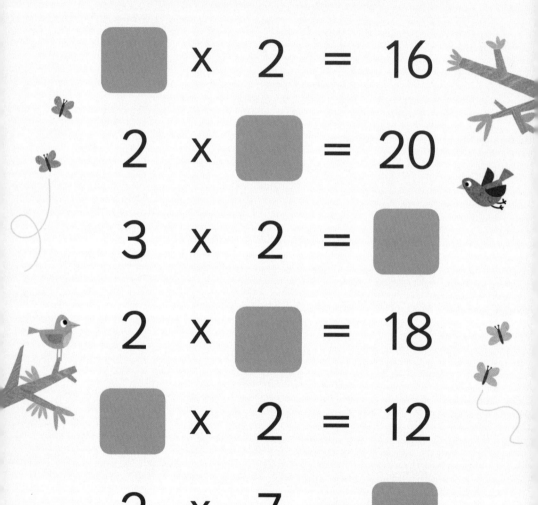

$\square \times 2 = 16$

$2 \times \square = 20$

$3 \times 2 = \square$

$2 \times \square = 18$

$\square \times 2 = 12$

$2 \times 7 = \square$

5 more

Draw more rows of 5 vegetables to fill this vegetable patch. Write how many vegetables there are in total at the end of each new row.

Row 1 — 5

Row 2 — 10

Row 3 — 15

Row 4 —

Row 5 —

I'm sure we planted more than 15...

5 more

Complete the other side of this page first.
Then finish writing each row as a calculation
from the 5 times table in the boxes below.

$$1 \times 5 = 5$$

$$\boxed{} \times \boxed{} = 10$$

$$\boxed{} \times \boxed{} = 15$$

$$\boxed{} \times \boxed{} = \boxed{}$$

$$\boxed{} \times \boxed{} = \boxed{}$$

Flower fives

Help Squilly count up the flowers in fives. Follow the arrows, and write the new total under each group.

5 → **10** → ☐ → ☐

I know that all of the numbers will end in a 5 or a 0.

Honeycomb

Find a route across the honeycomb. The next
cell's number must always be 5 more than
the number of the cell you are on.

Start

12 22
10 15 18 20 23
1 5 8 20 24 26 29
6 9 15 25 28 30
8 13 18 30 38 33 35
16 24 35 32 40 39
22 20 39 40 45 47 44
28 25 30 41 50
36 46

Finish

Sequences

49

Fill in the missing numbers in these sequences so that each number is 5 more than the one before.

5   [ ]   15   [ ]

20   [ ]   [ ]   35

10   [ ]   [ ]   25

25   [ ]   [ ]   [ ]

Sequences

Write the missing numbers in these sequences so that each number is 5 more than the one before.

15 | | | 30

30 | | | 45

10 | | 20 |

35 | | |

Adding in fives

For each calculation, count up the flowers in fives, then write the total number of flowers in the empty box.

✿✿ + ✿✿ = ☐

Now, let me see...

✿✿ + ✿✿ + ✿✿ = ☐

✿✿ + ✿✿ + ✿✿ + ✿✿ = ☐

✿✿ + ✿✿ + ✿✿ + ✿✿ + ✿✿ = ☐

Adding in fives

For each calculation, draw the final five flowers, then write the total number of flowers in the empty box.

$5 + 5 + 5 + 5 = \square$

$5 + 5 + 5 + 5 + 5 = \square$

$5 + 5 + 5 = \square$

What a lot of flowers!

$5 + 5 = \square$

Adding in fives

Help Foxy add up these numbers, and write the totals in the boxes.

$5 + 5 + 5 + 5 + 5 = $ ☐

$5 + 5 + 5 = $ ☐

$5 + 5 + 5 + 5 + 5 + 5 + 5 = $ ☐

$5 + 5 + 5 + 5 + 5 + 5 = $ ☐

5 10 15 20 25 30 35 40 45 50

Groups of 5

This group of 5 friends are going on a train journey. Write the numbers in the boxes at the bottom to finish the sentence.

1 group of 5 friends = ☐ friends altogether

5 10 15 20 25 30 35 40 45 50

Groups of 5

These groups of 5 friends are going on train journeys to different places. Write the numbers in the boxes at the bottom to finish the sentence.

2 groups of 5 friends = ☐ friends altogether

5   10   15   20   25   30   35   40   45   50

Groups of 5

Hug has found some groups of 5 fish to catch in his net. Circle each group, then write the numbers in the boxes at the bottom to finish the sentence.

3 groups of 5 fish = ☐ fish altogether

5   10   15   20   25   30   35   40   45   50

Groups of 5

Moley wants to catch these groups of 5 fish.
Circle each group, then write the numbers in
the boxes at the bottom to finish the sentence.

4 groups of 5 fish = ☐ fish altogether

5 10 15 20 25 30 35 40 45 50

Groups of 5

Stripe has collected these shells in groups of 5.
Circle each group, then write the numbers in the
boxes at the bottom to finish the sentence.

How many shells
have I got?

☐ groups of 5 shells = ☐ shells altogether

5 10 15 20 25 30 35 40 45 50

Groups of 5

Spike has arranged these shells into groups of 5.
Circle each group, then write the numbers in the
boxes at the bottom to finish the sentence.

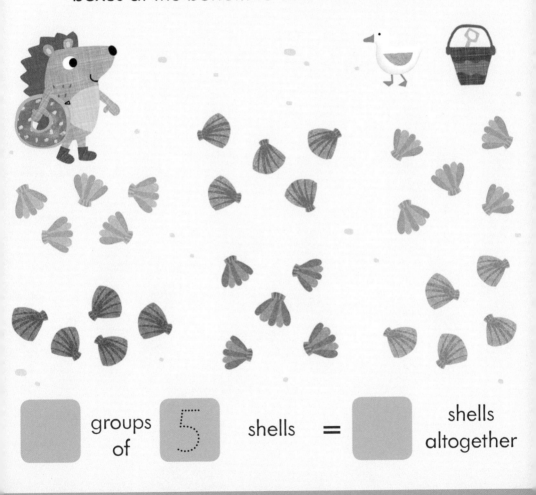

☐ groups of **5** shells = ☐ shells altogether

5 10 15 20 25 30 35 40 45 50

Groups of 5

Each of these friends has a bunch of 5 balloons.
Circle each bunch, then write the numbers in the
boxes at the bottom to finish the sentence.

[ ] bunches of **5** balloons = [ ] balloons altogether

(5) (10) (15) (20) (25) (30) (35) (40) (45) (50)

Groups of 5

Everyone here has a bunch of 5 balloons.
Circle each bunch, then write the numbers in
the boxes at the bottom to finish the sentence.

bunches of 5 balloons = balloons altogether

5 10 15 20 25 30 35 40 45 50

Groups of 5

Hug has arranged these cupcakes in groups of 5.
Circle each group, then write the numbers in the
boxes at the bottom to finish the sentence.

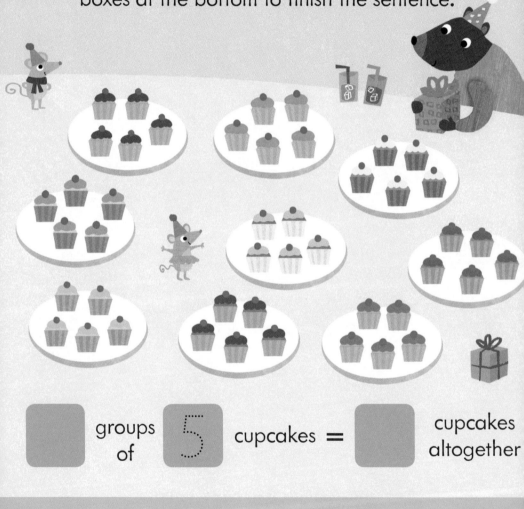

☐ groups of ⑤ cupcakes = ☐ cupcakes altogether

5 10 15 20 25 30 35 40 45 50

Groups of 5

Stripe has arranged these snacks in groups of 5.
Circle each group, then write the numbers in the
boxes at the bottom to finish the sentence.

Yum, yum!

☐ groups of 5 snacks = ☐ snacks altogether

5 10 15 20 25 30 35 40 45 50

Equal groups

Describe these groups in two different ways.
Write in the empty boxes how many groups there
are, and how many birds there are altogether.

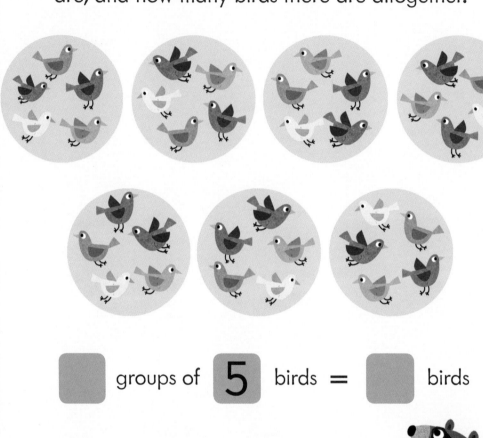

 groups of **5** birds = □ birds

□ x **5** = □ birds

Equal groups

Describe these groups in two different ways.
Write in the empty boxes how many groups there
are, and how many butterflies there are altogether.

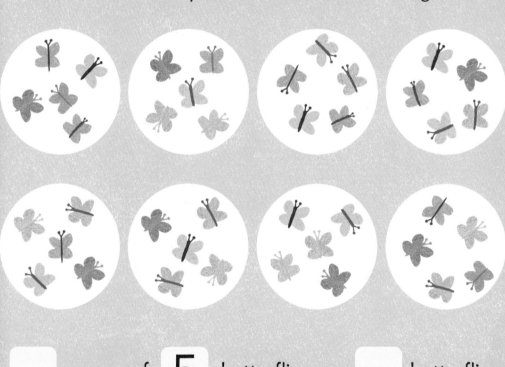

☐ groups of **5** butterflies = ☐ butterflies

☐ x **5** = ☐ butterflies

Equal groups

Describe these groups in two different ways.
Write in the empty boxes how many groups there
are, and how many bugs there are altogether.

 groups of bugs = bugs

 x 5 = bugs

Equal groups

Describe these groups in two different ways.
Write in the empty boxes how many groups there
are, and how many trees there are altogether.

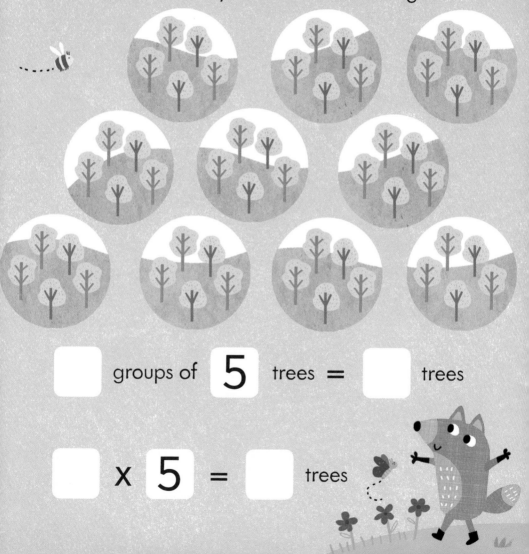

☐ groups of **5** trees = ☐ trees

☐ x **5** = ☐ trees

Equal groups

Describe these groups in two different ways.
Write in the empty boxes how many groups there
are, and how many clouds there are altogether.

[ ] groups of **5** clouds = [ ] clouds

[ ] x **5** = [ ] clouds

Equal groups

Describe this group in two different ways.
Write in the empty boxes how many groups there
are, and how many snails there are altogether.

☐ group of **5** snails = ☐ snails

☐ x **5** = ☐ snails

Equal groups

Describe these groups in two different ways.
Write in the empty boxes how many groups there
are, and how many gifts there are altogether.

☐ groups of **5** gifts = ☐ gifts

☐ x **5** = ☐ gifts

Equal groups

Describe these groups in two different ways.
Write in the empty boxes how many groups there
are, and how many cupcakes there are altogether.

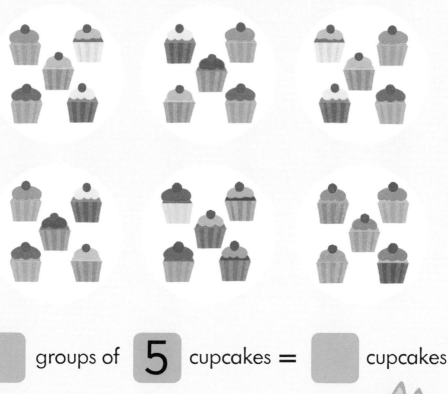

☐ groups of **5** cupcakes = ☐ cupcakes

☐ x **5** = ☐ cupcakes

Equal groups

Describe these groups in two different ways.
Write in the empty boxes how many groups there
are, and how many fish there are altogether.

☐ groups of **5** fish = ☐ fish

☐ x **5** = ☐ fish

Equal groups

Describe these groups in two different ways.
Write in the empty boxes how many groups there
are, and how many berries there are altogether.

☐ groups of **5** berries = ☐ berries

☐ x **5** = ☐ berries

Calculation pairs

Stripe and Squilly have been collecting berries. Fill in the numbers in the calculations below to see how many berries they each have, and to see if Squilly is right.

I think we both have the same number of berries, Stripe!

Stripe's calculation:

5 X 7 =

Squilly's calculation:

7 X 5 =

Calculation pairs

Fill in the blanks to complete two different calculations
for each group of fruit. One has been done for you.

...... x ...... = ...

...... x ...... = ...

4 x 5 = 20
5 x 4 = 20

...... x 5 = ...

...... x 6 = ...

5 x ...... = ...

2 x ...... = ...

Calculation pairs

Fill in the blanks to complete two different calculations for each group of berries. One has been done for you.

5 x 5 = 25
5 x 5 = 25

5 x ...... = ...
3 x ...... = ...

...... x 5 = ...
...... x 7 = ...

...... x ...... = ...
...... x ...... = ...

5 times table

Trace over the dotted numbers and fill in the empty boxes to finish these calculations in the 5 times table.

1 x 5 = ☐ | 6 x 5 = ☐

2 x 5 = ☐ | 7 x 5 = ☐

3 x 5 = ☐ | 8 x 5 = ☐

4 x 5 = ☐ | 9 x 5 = ☐

5 x 5 = ☐ | 10 x 5 = ☐

5 times table

Trace over the dotted numbers and fill in the empty boxes to finish these calculations in the 5 times table.

5 x 1 = ☐   5 x 6 = ☐

5 x 2 = ☐   5 x 7 = ☐

5 x 3 = ☐   5 x 8 = ☐

5 x 4 = ☐   5 x 9 = ☐

5 x 5 = ☐   5 x 10 = ☐

Calculation match-up

Help Foxy finish these calculations. Draw a
line to match each one to its answer.
One has been done for you.

5 x 3

25

8 x 5

20

40

30

5 x 7

5 x 9

35

4 x 5

15

5 x 6

45

5 x 5

How many fives?

Finish these forest calculations. To help, you could draw around groups of 5 trees until they are all in groups, then count the groups.

$$\boxed{} \times 5 = 5$$

$$\boxed{} \times 5 = 15$$

How many fives?

Complete these fish calculations. To help, you could draw around groups of 5 fish until they are all in groups, then count the groups.

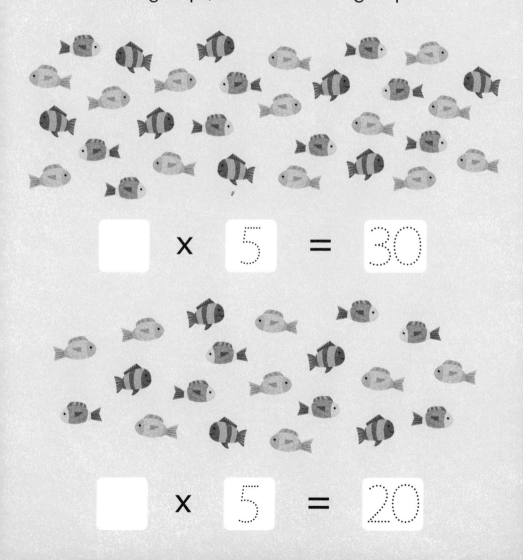

$$\boxed{} \times 5 = 30$$

$$\boxed{} \times 5 = 20$$

How many fives?

Finish these flower calculations. To help, you could draw around groups of 5 flowers until they are all in groups, then count the groups.

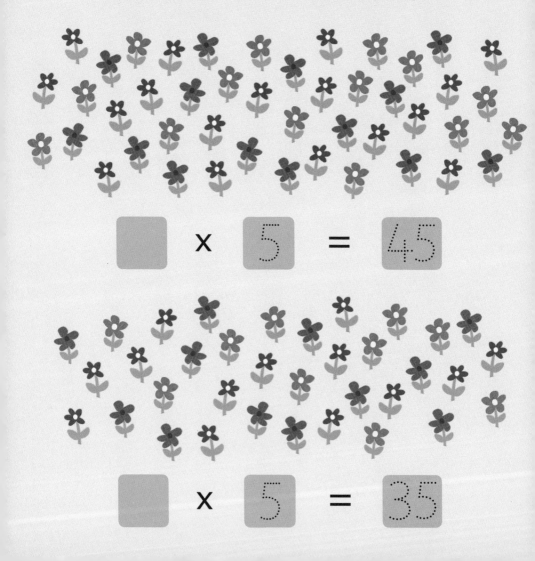

How many fives?

Complete these leaf calculations. To help, you could draw around groups of 5 leaves until they are all in groups, then count the groups.

$$\boxed{} \times \boxed{5} = \boxed{40}$$

What a lot of leaves!

$$\boxed{} \times \boxed{5} = \boxed{10}$$

How many fives?

Finish these snail calculations. To help, you could
draw around groups of 5 snails until they are
all in groups, then count the groups.

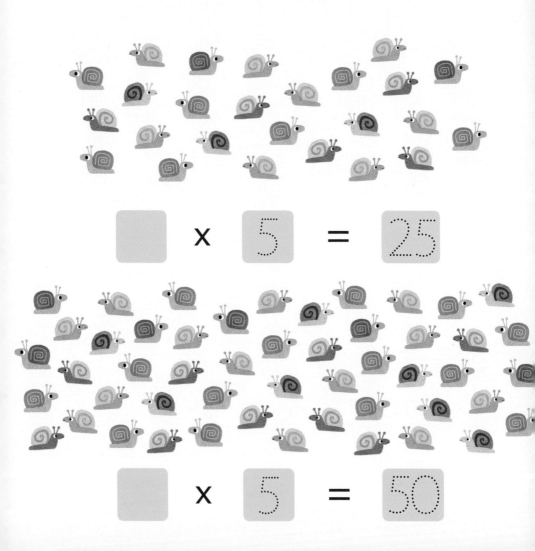

☐ x 5 = 25

☐ x 5 = 50

Missing numbers

Write the missing numbers in the boxes to finish these calculations from the 5 times table.

$\boxed{} \times 5 = 5$

$5 \times \boxed{} = 20$

$9 \times 5 = \boxed{}$

$5 \times \boxed{} = 35$

$\boxed{} \times 5 = 25$

$5 \times 2 = \boxed{}$

Missing numbers

Fill in the missing numbers in the boxes to finish these calculations from the 5 times table.

☐ x 5 = 30

5 x ☐ = 15

7 x 5 = ☐

5 x ☐ = 50

☐ x 5 = 20

5 x 8 = ☐

10 more

Draw more rows of 10 vegetables to fill this vegetable patch. Write how many vegetables there are in total at the end of each new row.

Row 1

10

Row 2

20

Row 3

30

Row 4

Row 5

Look at all our vegetables!

Complete the other side of this page first.
Then finish writing each row as a calculation
from the 10 times table in the boxes below.

1 x 10 = 10

x = 20

x = 30

x =

x =

Help Foxy count up the cupcakes in tens. Follow the
arrows, and write the new total under each group.

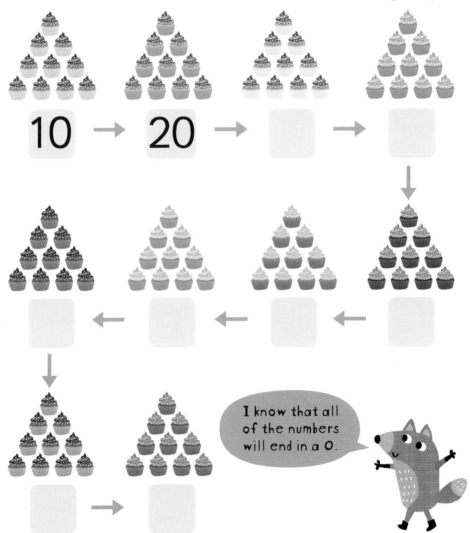

I know that all
of the numbers
will end in a O.

Honeycomb

Find a route across the honeycomb. The next cell's number must always be 10 more than the number of the cell you are on.

Start

20 30

15 28 40 52 62

18 10 25 36 45 60 71

20 35 50 50 58 70

28 30 40 60 64 72 84

37 41 70 69 78 82

45 52 60 80 88 90 89

61 71 85 90 100

92 99

Finish

Sequences

Fill in the missing numbers in these sequences so that each number is 10 more than the one before.

10   30

40   70

20   50

50

Sequences

Write the missing numbers in these sequences so that each number is 10 more than the one before.

30 [ ] [ ] 60

60 [ ] [ ] 90

20 [ ] 40 [ ]

70 [ ] [ ] [ ]

For each calculation, count up the leaves in tens, then write the total number of leaves in the empty box.

Look at all these lovely leaves, Mo!

Adding in tens

For each calculation, draw the final ten leaves, then
write the total number of leaves in the empty box.

10 + 10 + 10 + 10 = ☐

10 + 10 = ☐

10 + 10 + 10 = ☐

Adding in tens

Help Stripe add up these numbers,
and write the totals in the boxes.

10 + 10 + 10 + 10 + 10 + 10 + 10 + 10 =

10 + 10 + 10 =

10 + 10 + 10 + 10 + 10 =

10 + 10 + 10 + 10 + 10 + 10 =

10 20 30 40 50 60 70 80 90 100

Groups of 10

Hug has spotted a group of 10 bees.
Write the numbers in the boxes at
the bottom to finish the sentence.

1 group of 10 bees = bees altogether

10 20 30 40 50 60 70 80 90 100

Groups of 10

Moley has spotted some birds flying in flocks of 10. Circle each flock, then write the numbers in the boxes at the bottom to finish the sentence.

2 flocks of 10 birds = ☐ birds altogether

10 20 30 40 50 60 70 80 90 100

Groups of 10

Spike is watching some dragonflies flying in groups of 10. Circle each group, then write the numbers in the boxes at the bottom to finish the sentence.

3 groups of 10 dragonflies = ☐ dragonflies altogether

10 20 30 40 50 60 70 80 90 100

Groups of 10

Moley has seen some butterflies in groups of 10.
Circle each group, then write the numbers in
the boxes at the bottom to finish the sentence.

4 groups of 10 butterflies = ☐ butterflies altogether

10 20 30 40 50 60 70 80 90 100

Groups of 10

Hug has arranged these cupcakes in groups of 10.
Circle each group, then write the numbers in the
boxes at the bottom to finish the sentence.

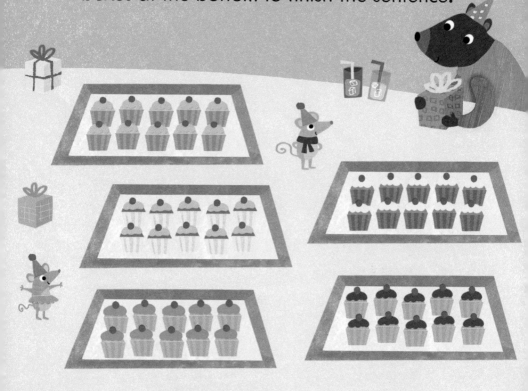

☐ groups of **10** cupcakes = ☐ cupcakes altogether

10 20 30 40 50 60 70 80 90 100

Groups of 10

Stripe has arranged these snacks in groups of 10.
Circle each group, then write the numbers in the
boxes at the bottom to finish the sentence.

Hope you're hungry, Mo!

☐ groups of 10 snacks = ☐ snacks altogether

10 20 30 40 50 60 70 80 90 100

Bun's found some groups of 10 fish to catch in her net. Circle each group, then write the numbers in the boxes at the bottom to finish the sentence.

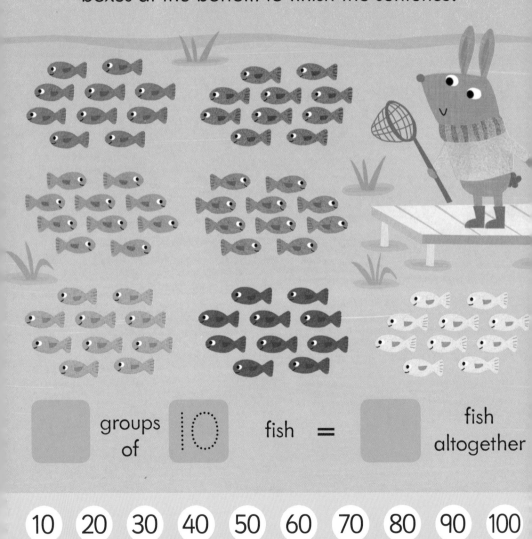

groups of 10   fish =   fish altogether

10 20 30 40 50 60 70 80 90 100

Groups of 10

Spike wants to catch these groups of 10 fish.
Circle each group, then write the numbers in
the boxes at the bottom to finish the sentence.

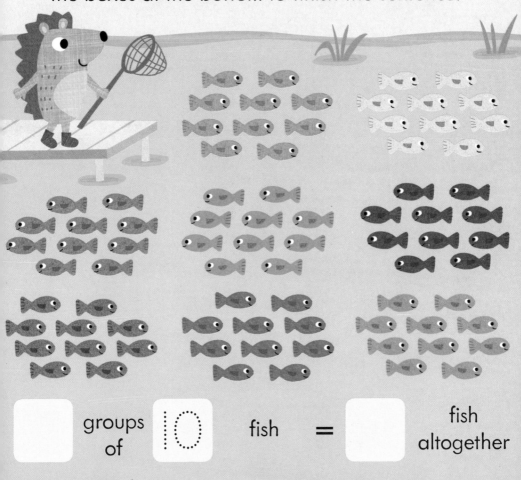

☐ groups of ⌜10⌝ fish = ☐ fish altogether

10 20 30 40 50 60 70 80 90 100

Groups of 10

Foxy and Bun are picking apples. They see there are 10 on each tree. Circle each tree, then write the numbers in the boxes at the bottom to finish the sentence.

[ ] trees with [10] apples = [ ] apples altogether

10   20   30   40   50   60   70   80   90   100

Groups of 10

Squilly and Stripe are picking apples from these trees.
Circle each tree's ten apples, then write the numbers
in the boxes at the bottom to finish the sentence.

[ ] trees with 10 apples = [ ] apples altogether

(10) (20) (30) (40) (50) (60) (70) (80) (90) (100)

Equal groups

Describe these groups in two different ways.
Write in the empty boxes how many groups there
are, and how many birds there are altogether.

[ ] groups of **10** birds = [ ] birds

[ ] **x 10** = [ ] birds

Equal groups

Describe these groups in two different ways.
Write in the empty boxes how many groups there
are, and how many butterflies there are altogether.

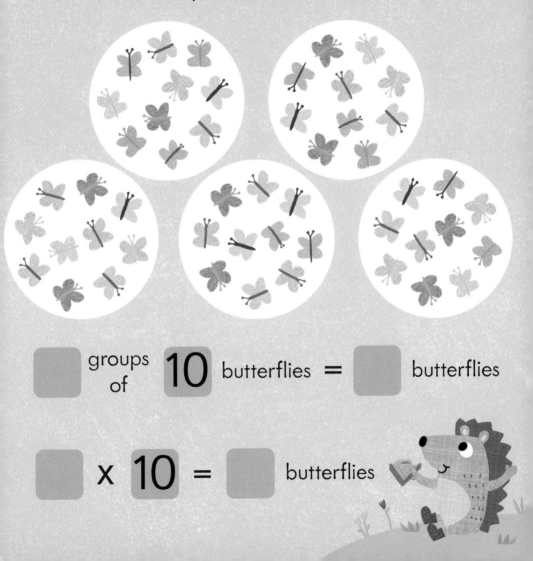

groups of **10** butterflies = butterflies

x **10** = butterflies

Equal groups

Describe these groups in two different ways.
Write in the empty boxes how many groups there
are, and how many flowers there are altogether.

☐ groups of **10** flowers = ☐ flowers

☐ x **10** = ☐ flowers

Equal groups

Describe these groups in two different ways.
Write in the empty boxes how many groups there
are, and how many worms there are altogether.

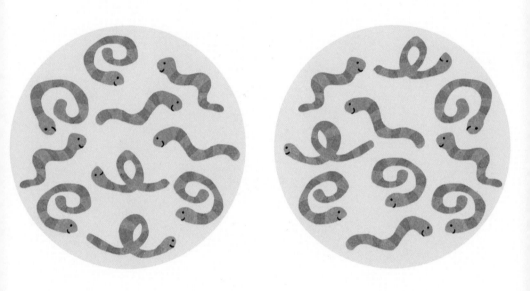

⬜ groups of **10** worms = ⬜ worms

⬜ **x** **10** = ⬜ worms

Equal groups

Describe this group in two different ways.
Write in the empty boxes how many groups there
are, and how many bugs there are altogether.

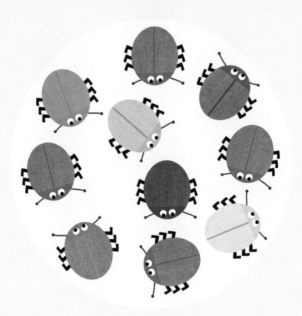

☐ group of **10** bugs = ☐ bugs

☐ x **10** = ☐ bugs

Equal groups

Describe these groups in two different ways.
Write in the empty boxes how many groups there
are, and how many acorns there are altogether.

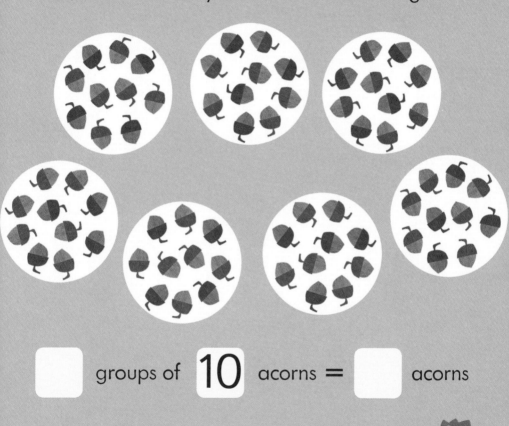

☐ groups of **10** acorns = ☐ acorns

☐ x **10** = ☐ acorns

Equal groups

Describe these groups in two different ways.
Write in the empty boxes how many groups there
are, and how many leaves there are altogether.

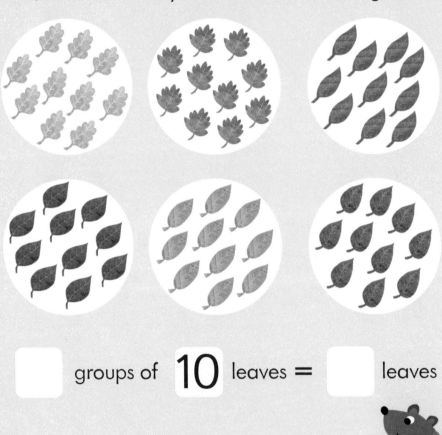

☐ groups of **10** leaves = ☐ leaves

☐ x **10** = ☐ leaves

Equal groups

Describe these groups in two different ways.
Write in the empty boxes how many groups there
are, and how many stars there are altogether.

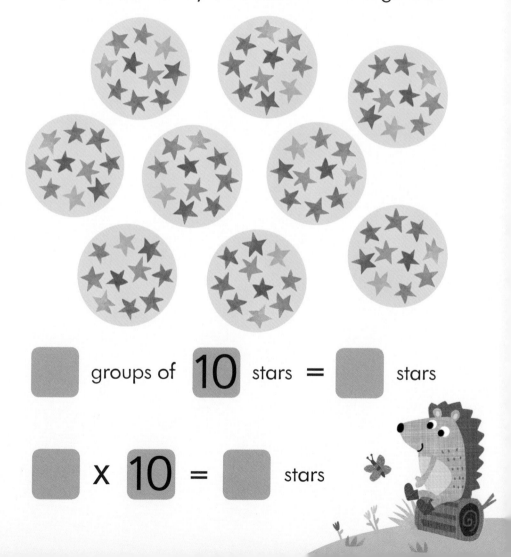

☐ groups of **10** stars = ☐ stars

☐ x **10** = ☐ stars

Equal groups

Describe these groups in two different ways. Write in the empty boxes how many groups there are, and how many pencils there are altogether.

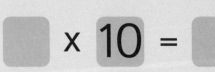 groups of **10** pencils = pencils

☐ x **10** = ☐ pencils

Equal groups

Describe these groups in two different ways. Write in the empty boxes how many groups there are, and how many balls there are altogether.

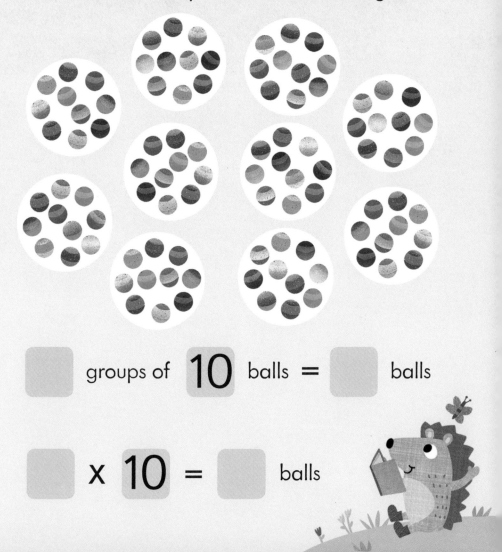

☐ groups of **10** balls = ☐ balls

☐ x **10** = ☐ balls

Calculation pairs

Stripe and Squilly have been picking peaches. Fill in the numbers in the calculations below to see how many peaches they each have, and to see if Squilly is right.

I think we both have the same number of peaches, Stripe!

Stripe's calculation: 10 x 4 =

Squilly's calculation: 4 x 10 =

Calculation pairs

Fill in the blanks to complete two different calculations for each group of balls. One has been done for you.

...... x 5 = ...
...... x 10 = ...

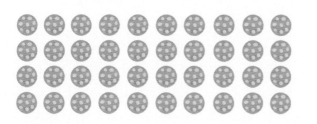

10 x 3 = 30
3 x 10 = 30

10 x ...... = ...
4 x ...... = ...

Calculation pairs

Fill in the blanks to complete two different calculations for each group of marbles. One has been done for you.

$$10 \times 6 = 60$$
$$6 \times 10 = 60$$

$$\text{......} \times 2 = \text{......}$$
$$\text{......} \times 10 = \text{......}$$

$$10 \times \text{......} = \text{......}$$
$$1 \times \text{......} = \text{......}$$

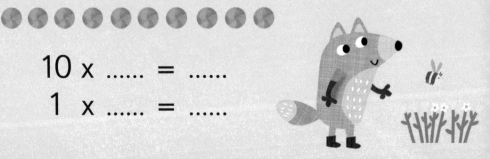

10 times table

Trace over the dotted numbers and fill in the empty boxes to finish these calculations in the 10 times table.

1 x 10 = ☐   6 x 10 = ☐

2 x 10 = ☐   7 x 10 = ☐

3 x 10 = ☐   8 x 10 = ☐

4 x 10 = ☐   9 x 10 = ☐

5 x 10 = ☐   10 x 10 = ☐

10 times table

Trace over the dotted numbers and fill in the empty boxes to finish these calculations in the 10 times table.

10 x 1 = ☐   10 x 6 = ☐

10 x 2 = ☐   10 x 7 = ☐

10 x 3 = ☐   10 x 8 = ☐

10 x 4 = ☐   10 x 9 = ☐

10 x 5 = ☐   10 x 10 = ☐

Calculation match-up

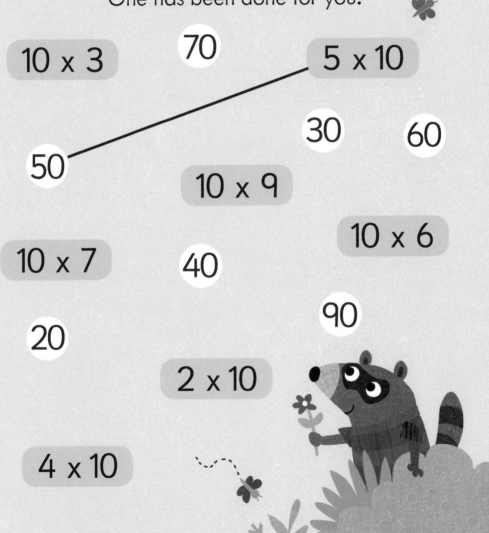

121

Help Coco finish these calculations. Draw a line to match each one to its answer. One has been done for you.

10 x 3

70

5 x 10

30   60

50

10 x 9

10 x 6

10 x 7   40

90

20

2 x 10

4 x 10

How many tens?

Finish these shell calculations. To help, you could draw around groups of 10 shells until they are all in groups, then count the groups.

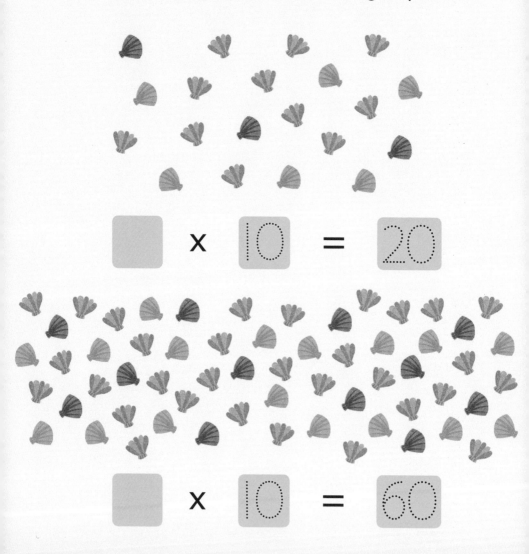

☐ x 10 = 20

☐ x 10 = 60

How many tens?

Complete these butterfly calculations. To help, you could draw around groups of 10 butterflies until they are all in groups, then count the groups.

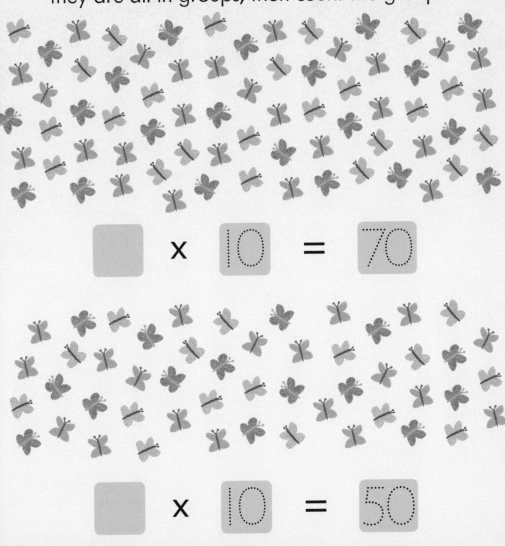

☐ × 10 = 70

☐ × 10 = 50

How many tens?

Finish these bee calculations. To help, you could draw around groups of 10 bees until they are all in groups, then count the groups.

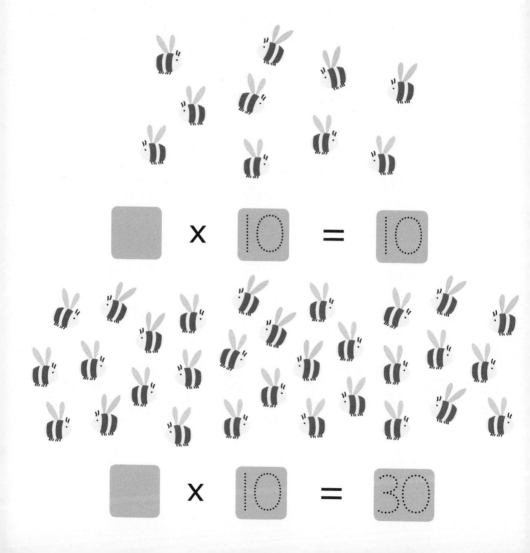

How many tens?

Complete these star calculations. To help, you could draw around groups of 10 stars until they are all in groups, then count the groups.

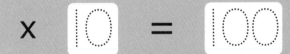

$$\boxed{} \times 10 = 100$$

$$\boxed{} \times 10 = 80$$

How many tens?

Finish these acorn calculations. To help, you could
draw around groups of 10 acorns until they
are all in groups, then count the groups.

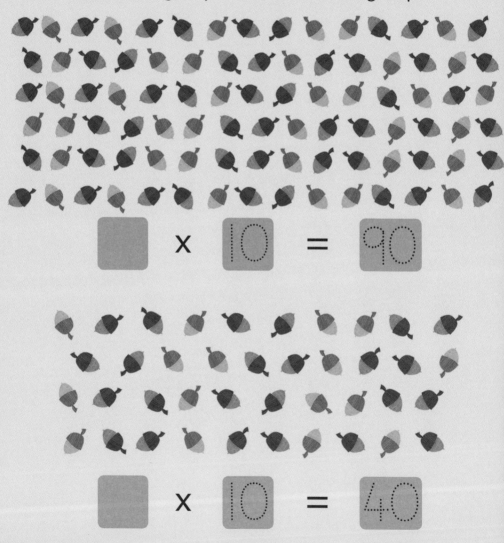

Missing numbers

Write the missing numbers in the boxes to finish these calculations from the 10 times table.

$\boxed{} \times 10 = 30$

$10 \times \boxed{} = 80$

$4 \times 10 = \boxed{}$

$10 \times \boxed{} = 70$

$\boxed{} \times 10 = 100$

$10 \times 1 = \boxed{}$

Missing numbers

Fill in the missing numbers in the boxes to finish these calculations from the 10 times table.

$\boxed{} \times 10 = 50$

$10 \times \boxed{} = 20$

$7 \times 10 = \boxed{}$

$10 \times \boxed{} = 90$

$\boxed{} \times 10 = 60$

$10 \times 10 = \boxed{}$

Mixed tables

Write the missing numbers in the boxes
to complete these calculations.

$\boxed{} \times 2 = 16$

$5 \times \boxed{} = 25$

$9 \times 10 = \boxed{}$

$7 \times \boxed{} = 14$

$\boxed{} \times 10 = 40$

$3 \times 5 = \boxed{}$

Mixed tables

Fill in the missing numbers in the boxes
to complete these calculations.

$\boxed{}$ x 5 = 30

4 x $\boxed{}$ = 8

8 x 10 = $\boxed{}$

5 x $\boxed{}$ = 10

$\boxed{}$ x 10 = 70

8 x 5 = $\boxed{}$

Mixed tables

Write the missing numbers in the boxes
to complete these calculations.

 x 2 = 6

2 x 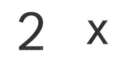 = 10

9 x 5 =

6 x  = 12

 x 10 = 30

4 x 5 =

Mixed tables

Fill in the missing numbers in the boxes
to complete these calculations.

 x 10 = 50

2 x  = 4

7 x 5 =

5 x  = 25

x 2 = 20

10 x 10 =

100 square

Help the mice finish drawing around the numbers
from the 2, 5 and 10 times tables in this 100 square.

1	②	3	④	5	⑥	7	8	9	10
11	12	13	14	15	16	17	18	19	20
21	22	23	24	25	26	27	28	29	30
31	32	33	34	35	36	37	38	39	40
41	42	43	44	45	46	47	48	49	50
51	52	53	54	55	56	57	58	59	60
61	62	63	64	65	66	67	68	69	70
71	72	73	74	75	76	77	78	79	80
81	82	83	84	85	86	87	88	89	90
91	92	93	94	95	96	97	98	99	100

Help me circle the rest of the
numbers in the 2 times table.

Can you draw a triangle
around each number in the
5 times table for me?

Please draw
squares around
the numbers in the
10 times table.

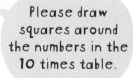

The 2 times table

Coco and Spike have written out the 2 times table below to help you to learn and remember it.

1 x 2 = 2

2 x 2 = 4

3 x 2 = 6

4 x 2 = 8

5 x 2 = 10

6 x 2 = 12

7 x 2 = 14

8 x 2 = 16

9 x 2 = 18

10 x 2 = 20

The 5 times table

Coco and Spike have written out the 5 times table below to help you to learn and remember it.

1 x 5 = 5

7 x 5 = 35

2 x 5 = 10

8 x 5 = 40

3 x 5 = 15

9 x 5 = 45

4 x 5 = 20

10 x 5 = 50

5 x 5 = 25

6 x 5 = 30

The 10 times table

Coco and Spike have written out the 10 times table below to help you to learn and remember it.

1 x 10 = 10

2 x 10 = 20

3 x 10 = 30

4 x 10 = 40

5 x 10 = 50

6 x 10 = 60

7 x 10 = 70

8 x 10 = 80

9 x 10 = 90

10 x 10 = 100

Answers

2 more · 1

Count the berries in each group below, then draw 2 more. Write the numbers in the boxes.

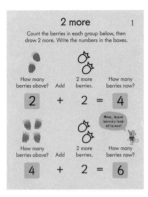

How many berries above? **2** Add **+** 2 more berries. **2** How many berries now? **= 4**

How many berries above? **4** Add **+** 2 more berries. **2** How many berries now? **= 6**

Mmm, those berries look delicious!

2 more · 2

Count the shells in each group below, then draw 2 more. Write the numbers in the boxes.

How many shells above? **6** Add **+** 2 more shells. **2** How many shells now? **= 8**

How many shells above? **8** Add **+** 2 more shells. **2** How many shells now? **= 10**

2 more · 3

Count the balls in each group below, then draw 2 more. Write the numbers in the boxes.

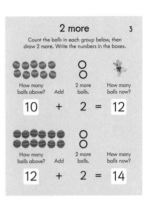

How many balls above? **10** Add **+** 2 more balls. **2** How many balls now? **= 12**

How many balls above? **12** Add **+** 2 more balls. **2** How many balls now? **= 14**

2 more · 4

Count the berries in each group below, then draw 2 more. Write the numbers in the boxes.

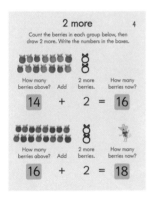

How many berries above? **14** Add **+** 2 more berries. **2** How many berries now? **= 16**

How many berries above? **16** Add **+** 2 more berries. **2** How many berries now? **= 18**

Sock twos · 5

Help Spike count up the socks in twos. Follow the arrows, and write the new total under each group.

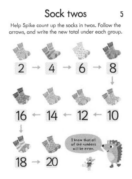

2 → 4 → 6 → 8

16 ← 14 ← 12 ← 10

18 → 20

I know that all of the numbers will be even.

Honeycomb · 6

Find a route across the honeycomb. The next cell's number must always be 2 more than the number of the cell you are on.

Sequences · 7

Fill in the missing numbers in these sequences so that each number is 2 more than the one before.

2 4 6 8

12 14 16 18

4 6 8 10

8 10 12 14

Sequences · 8

Write the missing numbers in these sequences so that each number is 2 more than the one before.

6 8 10 12

10 12 14 16

4 6 8 10

14 16 18 20

Adding in twos · 9

For each calculation, count up the socks in twos, then write the total number of socks in the empty box.

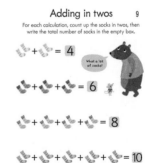

+ = 4

What a lot of socks!

+ + = 6

+ + + = 8

+ + + + = 10

Answers

Adding in twos 10

For each calculation, draw the final two socks, then write the total number of socks in the empty box.

$2 + 2 + 2 + 2 + 2 = 10$

$2 + 2 + 2 = 6$

That's a big yon, Mo!

$2 + 2 = 4$

$2 + 2 + 2 + 2 = 8$

Adding in twos 11

Help Moley add up these numbers, and write the totals in the boxes.

$2 + 2 + 2 = 6$

Hold it steady, Stripe!

$2 + 2 + 2 + 2 + 2 = 10$

$2 + 2 + 2 + 2 + 2 + 2 = 12$

$2 + 2 + 2 + 2 + 2 + 2 + 2 = 14$

2 4 6 8 10 12 14 16 18 20

Groups of 2 12

Spike and his friend are taking a nature walk. Trace over the numbers in the boxes at the bottom to finish the sentence.

Nice day for a walk, Spike!

1 group of **2** friends = **2** friends altogether

2 4 6 8 10 12 14 16 18 20

Groups of 2 13

A pair of friends have joined the hedgehogs' walk. Write the numbers in the boxes at the bottom to finish the sentence.

Good to see you, Spike!

2 groups of **2** friends = **4** friends altogether

2 4 6 8 10 12 14 16 18 20

Groups of 2 14

A pair of moles have joined the hedgehogs and raccoons on their walk. Write the numbers in the boxes at the bottom to finish the sentence.

Are we nearly there?

3 groups of **2** friends = **6** friends altogether

2 4 6 8 10 12 14 16 18 20

Groups of 2 15

Moley has spotted some butterflies in groups of 2. Circle each group, then write the numbers in the boxes at the bottom to finish the sentence.

Those butterflies are pretty!

4 groups of **2** butterflies = **8** butterflies altogether

2 4 6 8 10 12 14 16 18 20

Groups of 2 16

Moley is watching these groups of 2 butterflies. Circle each group, then write the numbers in the boxes at the bottom to finish the sentence.

5 groups of **2** butterflies = **10** butterflies altogether

2 4 6 8 10 12 14 16 18 20

Groups of 2 17

Hug has spotted some dragonflies flying in groups of 2. Circle each group, then write the numbers in the boxes at the bottom to finish the sentence.

How many dragonflies are there?

6 groups of **2** dragonflies = **12** dragonflies altogether

2 4 6 8 10 12 14 16 18 20

Groups of 2 18

Hug is watching these groups of 2 dragonflies. Circle each group, then write the numbers in the boxes at the bottom to finish the sentence.

There are lots of dragonflies around today!

7 groups of **2** dragonflies = **14** dragonflies altogether

2 4 6 8 10 12 14 16 18 20

Answers

Groups of 2 19

Coco has spotted some birds in groups of 2.
Circle each group, then write the numbers in
the boxes at the bottom to finish the sentence.

8 groups of 2 birds = 16 birds altogether

2 4 6 8 10 12 14 16 18 20

Groups of 2 20

Coco is watching these groups of 2 birds.
Circle each group, then write the numbers in
the boxes at the bottom to finish the sentence.

9 groups of 2 birds = 18 birds altogether

2 4 6 8 10 12 14 16 18 20

Groups of 2 21

Foxy has spotted some bees in groups of 2.
Circle each group, then write the numbers in
the boxes at the bottom to finish the sentence.

10 groups of 2 bees = 20 bees altogether

2 4 6 8 10 12 14 16 18 20

Equal groups 22

Describe these groups in two different ways.
Write in the empty boxes how many groups there
are, and how many snails there are altogether.

6 groups of 2 snails = 12 snails

6 x 2 = 12 snails

Equal groups 23

Describe these groups in two different ways.
Write in the empty boxes how many groups there
are, and how many leaves there are altogether.

9 groups of 2 leaves = 18 leaves

9 x 2 = 18 leaves

Equal groups 24

Describe these groups in two different ways.
Write in the empty boxes how many groups there
are, and how many snakes there are altogether.

2 groups of 2 snakes = 4 snakes

2 x 2 = 4 snakes

Equal groups 25

Describe this group in two different ways.
Write in the empty boxes how many groups there
are, and how many trees there are altogether.

1 group of 2 trees = 2 trees

1 x 2 = 2 trees

Equal groups 26

Describe these groups in two different ways.
Write in the empty boxes how many groups there
are, and how many clouds there are altogether.

3 groups of 2 clouds = 6 clouds

3 x 2 = 6 clouds

Equal groups 27

Describe these groups in two different ways.
Write in the empty boxes how many groups there
are, and how many kites there are altogether.

4 groups of 2 kites = 8 kites

Hello, little bee

4 x 2 = 8 kites

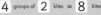

Answers

Equal groups 28

Describe these groups in two different ways. Write in the empty boxes how many groups there are, and how many flowers there are altogether.

5 groups of 2 flowers = 10 flowers

5 x 2 = 10 flowers

Equal groups 29

Describe these groups in two different ways. Write in the empty boxes how many groups there are, and how many shells there are altogether.

7 groups of 2 shells = 14 shells

7 x 2 = 14 shells

Equal groups 30

Describe these groups in two different ways. Write in the empty boxes how many groups there are, and how many fish there are altogether.

8 groups of 2 fish = 16 fish

8 x 2 = 16 fish

Equal groups 31

Describe these groups in two different ways. Write in the empty boxes how many groups there are, and how many stars there are altogether.

10 groups of 2 stars = 20 stars

10 x 2 = 20 stars

Calculation pairs 32

Stripe and Squilly have been collecting acorns. Fill in the numbers in the calculations below to see how many acorns they each have, and to see if Squilly is right.

I think we both have the same number of acorns, Stripe!

Stripe's calculation: 2 x 9 = 18

Squilly's calculation: 9 x 2 = 18

Calculation pairs 33

Fill in the blanks to complete two different calculations for each group of toys. One has been done for you.

10 x 2 = 20
2 x 10 = 20

3 x 2 = 6
2 x 3 = 6

5 x 2 = 10
2 x 5 = 10

6 x 2 = 12
2 x 6 = 12

Calculation pairs 34

Fill in the blanks to complete two different calculations for each group of animals. One has been done for you.

4 x 2 = 8
2 x 4 = 8

2 x 2 = 4
2 x 2 = 4

7 x 2 = 14
2 x 7 = 14

9 x 2 = 18
2 x 9 = 18

2 times table 35

Trace over the dotted numbers and fill in the empty boxes to finish these calculations in the 2 times table.

1 x 2 = 2   6 x 2 = 12

2 x 2 = 4   7 x 2 = 14

3 x 2 = 6   8 x 2 = 16

4 x 2 = 8   9 x 2 = 18

5 x 2 = 10   10 x 2 = 20

2 times table 36

Trace over the dotted numbers and fill in the empty boxes to finish these calculations in the 2 times table.

2 x 1 = 2   2 x 6 = 12

2 x 2 = 4   2 x 7 = 14

2 x 3 = 6   2 x 8 = 16

2 x 4 = 8   2 x 9 = 18

2 x 5 = 10   2 x 10 = 20

Answers

Calculation match-up 37

Help Bun finish these calculations. Draw a line to match each one to its answer. One has been done for you.

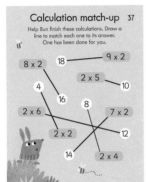

8 x 2 — 18 — 9 x 2
4 — 2 x 5 — 10
2 x 6 — 16 — 8
2 x 2 — 7 x 2
14 — 2 x 4 — 12

How many twos? 38

Finish these calculations for Stripe and Squilly. To help, you could draw around groups of 2 blossoms until they are all in groups, then count the groups.

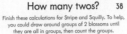

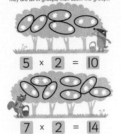

5 × 2 = 10

7 × 2 = 14

How many twos? 39

Complete these calculations for Stripe and Squilly. To help, you could draw around groups of 2 cherries until they are all in groups, then count the groups.

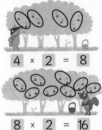

4 × 2 = 8

8 × 2 = 16

How many twos? 40

Finish these calculations for Stripe and Squilly. To help, you could draw around groups of 2 apples until they are all in groups, then count the groups.

6 × 2 = 12

1 × 2 = 2

How many twos? 41

Complete these calculations for Stripe and Squilly. To help, you could draw around groups of 2 acorns until they are all in groups, then count the groups.

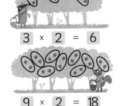

3 × 2 = 6

9 × 2 = 18

How many twos? 42

Finish these calculations for Stripe and Squilly. To help, you could draw around groups of 2 plums until they are all in groups, then count the groups.

2 × 2 = 4

10 × 2 = 20

Missing numbers 43

Write the missing numbers in the boxes to finish these calculations from the 2 times table.

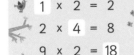

1 x 2 = 2
2 x 4 = 8
9 x 2 = 18
2 x 7 = 14
2 x 2 = 4
2 x 5 = 10

Missing numbers 44

Fill in the missing numbers in the boxes to finish these calculations from the 2 times table.

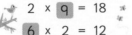

8 x 2 = 16
2 x 10 = 20
3 x 2 = 6
2 x 9 = 18
6 x 2 = 12
2 x 7 = 14

5 more 45

Draw more rows of 5 vegetables to fill this vegetable patch. Write how many vegetables there are in total at the end of each new row.

Row 1 — 5
Row 2 — 10
Row 3 — 15
Row 4 — 20
Row 5 — 25

I'm sure we planted more than 15.

Answers

5 more   46

Complete the other side of this page first.
Then finish writing each row as a calculation
from the 5 times table in the boxes below.

$1 \times 5 = 5$

$2 \times 5 = 10$

$3 \times 5 = 15$

$4 \times 5 = 20$

$5 \times 5 = 25$

Flower fives   47

Help Squilly count up the flowers in fives. Follow the
arrows, and write the new total under each group.

$5 \rightarrow 10 \rightarrow 15 \rightarrow 20$

$40 \leftarrow 35 \leftarrow 30 \leftarrow 25$

I know that all
of the numbers
will end in a
5 or a 0.

$45 \rightarrow 50$

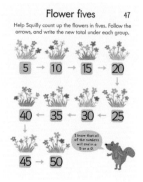

Honeycomb   48

Find a route across the honeycomb. The next
cell's number must always be 5 more than
the number of the cell you are on.

Start

	12	22			
10	15	18	20	23	
1	5	8	13	24	26	29
6	9	15	25	28	30	
8	13	18	30	38	33	35
16	24	36	32	40	39	
22	20	39	40	45	47	44
28	25	30	41	50	
	36	46			

Finish

Sequences   49

Fill in the missing numbers in these sequences so
that each number is 5 more than the one before.

| 5 | 10 | 15 | 20 |

| 20 | 25 | 30 | 35 |

| 10 | 15 | 20 | 25 |

| 25 | 30 | 35 | 40 |

Sequences   50

Write the missing numbers in these sequences so
that each number is 5 more than the one before.

| 15 | 20 | 25 | 30 |

| 30 | 35 | 40 | 45 |

| 10 | 15 | 20 | 25 |

| 35 | 40 | 45 | 50 |

Adding in fives   51

For each calculation, count up the flowers in fives, then
write the total number of flowers in the empty box.

$+ = 10$

Now, let
me see...

$+ + = 15$

$+ + + = 20$

$+ + + + = 25$

Adding in fives   52

For each calculation, draw the final five flowers, then
write the total number of flowers in the empty box.

$5 + 5 + 5 + 5 = 20$

$5 + 5 + 5 + 5 + 5 = 25$

$5 + 5 + 5 = 15$

What a lot
of flowers!

$5 + 5 = 10$

Adding in fives   53

Help Foxy add up these numbers,
and write the totals in the boxes.

$5 + 5 + 5 + 5 + 5 = 25$

$5 + 5 + 5 = 15$

$5 + 5 + 5 + 5 + 5 + 5 + 5 = 35$

$5 + 5 + 5 + 5 + 5 + 5 = 30$

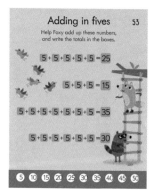

5 10 15 20 25 30 35 40 45 50

Groups of 5   54

This group of 5 friends are going on a train
journey. Write the numbers in the boxes
at the bottom to finish the sentence.

| 1 | group of | 5 | friends = | 5 | friends altogether |

5 10 15 20 25 30 35 40 45 50

Answers

Groups of 5   55

These groups of 5 friends are going on train journeys to different places. Write the numbers in the boxes at the bottom to finish the sentence.

`2` groups of `5` friends = `10` friends altogether

5 10 15 20 25 30 35 40 45 50

Groups of 5   56

Hug has found some groups of 5 fish to catch in his net. Circle each group, then write the numbers in the boxes at the bottom to finish the sentence.

`3` groups of `5` fish = `15` fish altogether

5 10 15 20 25 30 35 40 45 50

Groups of 5   57

Moley wants to catch these groups of 5 fish. Circle each group, then write the numbers in the boxes at the bottom to finish the sentence.

`4` groups of `5` fish = `20` fish altogether

(5) 10 (15) (20) (25) 30 (35) 40 (45) (50)

Groups of 5   58

Stripe has collected these shells in groups of 5. Circle each group, then write the numbers in the boxes at the bottom to finish the sentence.

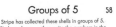

`5` groups of `5` shells = `25` shells altogether

(5) 10 (15) 20 (25) 30 (35) 40 (45) 50

Groups of 5   59

Spike has arranged these shells into groups of 5. Circle each group, then write the numbers in the boxes at the bottom to finish the sentence.

`6` groups of `5` shells = `30` shells altogether

5 10 15 20 25 30 35 40 45 50

Groups of 5   60

Each of these friends has a bunch of 5 balloons. Circle each bunch, then write the numbers in the boxes at the bottom to finish the sentence.

`7` bunches of `5` balloons = `35` balloons altogether

(5) (10) (15) (20) (25) (30) (35) 40 (45) 50

Groups of 5   61

Everyone here has a bunch of 5 balloons. Circle each bunch, then write the numbers in the boxes at the bottom to finish the sentence.

`8` bunches of `5` balloons = `40` balloons altogether

(5) 10 (15) (20) (25) 30 (35) (40) 45 (50)

Groups of 5   62

Hug has arranged these cupcakes in groups of 5. Circle each group, then write the numbers in the boxes at the bottom to finish the sentence.

`9` groups of `5` cupcakes = `45` cupcakes altogether

5 10 15 20 25 30 35 40 45 50

Groups of 5   63

Stripe has arranged these snacks in groups of 5. Circle each group, then write the numbers in the boxes at the bottom to finish the sentence.

`10` groups of `5` snacks = `50` snacks altogether

(5) (10) (15) (20) (25) (30) (35) (40) 45 (50)

Answers

Equal groups   64

Describe these groups in two different ways.
Write in the empty boxes how many groups there
are, and how many birds there are altogether.

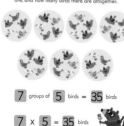

7 groups of 5 birds = 35 birds

7 x 5 = 35 birds

Equal groups   65

Describe these groups in two different ways.
Write in the empty boxes how many groups there
are, and how many butterflies there are altogether.

8 groups of 5 butterflies = 40 butterflies

8 x 5 = 40 butterflies

Equal groups   66

Describe these groups in two different ways.
Write in the empty boxes how many groups there
are, and how many bugs there are altogether.

4 groups of 5 bugs = 20 bugs

4 x 5 = 20 bugs

Equal groups   67

Describe these groups in two different ways.
Write in the empty boxes how many groups there
are, and how many trees there are altogether.

10 groups of 5 trees = 50 trees

10 x 5 = 50 trees

Equal groups   68

Describe these groups in two different ways.
Write in the empty boxes how many groups there
are, and how many clouds there are altogether.

5 groups of 5 clouds = 25 clouds

5 x 5 = 25 clouds

Equal groups   69

Describe this group in two different ways.
Write in the empty boxes how many groups there
are, and how many snails there are altogether.

1 group of 5 snails = 5 snails

1 x 5 = 5 snails

Equal groups   70

Describe these groups in two different ways.
Write in the empty boxes how many groups there
are, and how many gifts there are altogether.

3 groups of 5 gifts = 15 gifts

3 x 5 = 15 gifts

Equal groups   71

Describe these groups in two different ways.
Write in the empty boxes how many groups there
are, and how many cupcakes there are altogether.

6 groups of 5 cupcakes = 30 cupcakes

6 x 5 = 30 cupcakes

Equal groups   72

Describe these groups in two different ways.
Write in the empty boxes how many groups there
are, and how many fish there are altogether.

2 groups of 5 fish = 10 fish

2 x 5 = 10 fish

Answers

Equal groups 73

Describe these groups in two different ways.
Write in the empty boxes how many groups there
are, and how many berries there are altogether.

9 groups of **5** berries = **45** berries

9 x **5** = **45** berries

Calculation pairs 74

Stripe and Squilly have been collecting berries. Fill in
the numbers in the calculations below to see how many
berries they each have, and to see if Squilly is right.

I think we both have
the same number of
berries, Stripe!

Stripe's
calculation: **5** x **7** = **35**

Squilly's
calculation: **7** x **5** = **35**

Calculation pairs 75

Fill in the blanks to complete two different calculations
for each group of fruit. One has been done for you.

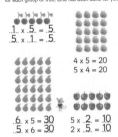

1 x **5** = **5**
5 x **1** = **5**

4 x 5 = 20
5 x 4 = 20

6 x 5 = **30**
5 x 6 = **30**

5 x **2** = **10**
2 x **5** = **10**

Calculation pairs 76

Fill in the blanks to complete two different calculations
for each group of berries. One has been done for you.

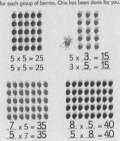

5 x 5 = 25
5 x 5 = 25

5 x **3** = **15**
3 x **5** = **15**

7 x 5 = 35
5 x 7 = 35

8 x **5** = **40**
5 x **8** = **40**

5 times table 77

Trace over the dotted numbers and fill in the empty
boxes to finish these calculations in the 5 times table.

1 x **5** = **5**   **6** x **5** = **30**

2 x **5** = **10**   **7** x **5** = **35**

3 x **5** = **15**   **8** x **5** = **40**

4 x **5** = **20**   **9** x **5** = **45**

5 x **5** = **25**   **10** x **5** = **50**

5 times table 78

Trace over the dotted numbers and fill in the empty
boxes to finish these calculations in the 5 times table.

5 x **1** = **5**   **5** x **6** = **30**

5 x **2** = **10**   **5** x **7** = **35**

5 x **3** = **15**   **5** x **8** = **40**

5 x **4** = **20**   **5** x **9** = **45**

5 x **5** = **25**   **5** x **10** = **50**

Calculation match-up 79

Help Foxy finish these calculations. Draw a
line to match each one to its answer.
One has been done for you.

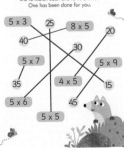

5 x 3   25   8 x 5   20
40   30
5 x 7   5 x 9
35   4 x 5   15
5 x 6   45
5 x 5

How many fives? 80

Finish these forest calculations. To help, you could
draw around groups of 5 trees until they are
all in groups, then count the groups.

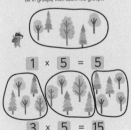

1 x **5** = **5**

3 x **5** = **15**

How many fives? 81

Complete these fish calculations. To help, you could
draw around groups of 5 fish until they are
all in groups, then count the groups.

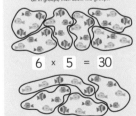

6 x **5** = **30**

4 x **5** = **20**

Answers

How many fives? 82

Finish these flower calculations. To help, you could draw around groups of 5 flowers until they are all in groups, then count the groups.

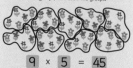

$9 \times 5 = 45$

$7 \times 5 = 35$

How many fives? 83

Complete these leaf calculations. To help, you could draw around groups of 5 leaves until they are all in groups, then count the groups.

$8 \times 5 = 40$

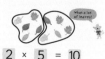

What a lot of leaves!

$2 \times 5 = 10$

How many fives? 84

Finish these snail calculations. To help, you could draw around groups of 5 snails until they are all in groups, then count the groups.

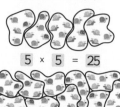

$5 \times 5 = 25$

$10 \times 5 = 50$

Missing numbers 85

Write the missing numbers in the boxes to finish these calculations from the 5 times table.

$1 \times 5 = 5$

$5 \times 4 = 20$

$9 \times 5 = 45$

$5 \times 7 = 35$

$5 \times 5 = 25$

$5 \times 2 = 10$

Missing numbers 86

Fill in the missing numbers in the boxes to finish these calculations from the 5 times table.

$6 \times 5 = 30$

$5 \times 3 = 15$

$7 \times 5 = 35$

$5 \times 10 = 50$

$4 \times 5 = 20$

$5 \times 8 = 40$

10 more 87

Draw more rows of 10 vegetables to fill this vegetable patch. Write how many vegetables there are in total at the end of each new row.

Row 1 — 10
Row 2 — 20
Row 3 — 30
Row 4 — 40
Row 5 — 50

Look at all our vegetables!

10 more 88

Complete the other side of this page first. Then finish writing each row as a calculation from the 10 times table in the boxes below.

$1 \times 10 = 10$

$2 \times 10 = 20$

$3 \times 10 = 30$

$4 \times 10 = 40$

$5 \times 10 = 50$

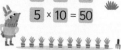

Cupcake tens 89

Help Foxy count up the cupcakes in tens. Follow the arrows, and write the new total under each group.

$10 \rightarrow 20 \rightarrow 30 \rightarrow 40$

$80 \leftarrow 70 \leftarrow 60 \leftarrow 50$

$90 \rightarrow 100$

I know that all of the numbers will end in a 0.

Honeycomb 90

Find a route across the honeycomb. The next cell's number must always be 10 more than the number of the cell you are on.

Start

20   30
15   28   40   52   62
18   10   25   36   45   60   71
20   35   50   50   58   70
28   30   40   60   64   72   84
37   41   70   69   78   82
45   52   60   80   79   80   89
61   71   85   90   100

92   99
Finish

Answers

Sequences 91

Fill in the missing numbers in these sequences so that each number is 10 more than the one before.

10 20 30 40

40 50 60 70

20 30 40 50

50 60 70 80

Sequences 92

Write the missing numbers in these sequences so that each number is 10 more than the one before.

30 40 50 60

60 70 80 90

20 30 40 50

70 80 90 100

Adding in tens 93

For each calculation, count up the leaves in tens, then write the total number of leaves in the empty box.

Look at all these lovely leaves, Ma!

+ = 20

+ + = 30

+ + + = 40

Adding in tens 94

For each calculation, draw the final ten leaves, then write the total number of leaves in the empty box.

10 + 10 + 10 + 10 = 40

10 + 10 = 20

10 + 10 + 10 = 30

Adding in tens 95

Help Stripe add up these numbers, and write the totals in the boxes.

10 + 10 + 10 + 10 + 10 + 10 + 10 + 10 = 80

10 + 10 + 10 = 30

10 + 10 + 10 + 10 + 10 = 50

10 + 10 + 10 + 10 + 10 + 10 = 60

10 20 30 40 50 60 70 80 90 100

Groups of 10 96

Hug has spotted a group of 10 bees. Write the numbers in the boxes at the bottom to finish the sentence.

1 group of 10 bees = 10 bees altogether

10 20 30 40 50 60 70 80 90 100

Groups of 10 97

Moley has spotted some birds flying in flocks of 10. Circle each flock, then write the numbers in the boxes at the bottom to finish the sentence.

2 flocks of 10 birds = 20 birds altogether

10 20 30 40 50 60 70 80 90 100

Groups of 10 98

Spike is watching some dragonflies flying in groups of 10. Circle each group, then write the numbers in the boxes at the bottom to finish the sentence.

3 groups of 10 dragonflies = 30 dragonflies altogether

10 20 30 40 50 60 70 80 90 100

Groups of 10 99

Moley has seen some butterflies in groups of 10. Circle each group, then write the numbers in the boxes at the bottom to finish the sentence.

4 groups of 10 butterflies = 40 butterflies altogether

10 20 30 40 50 60 70 80 90 100

Answers

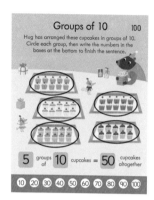

Groups of 10 — 100

Hug has arranged these cupcakes in groups of 10. Circle each group, then write the numbers in the boxes at the bottom to finish the sentence.

5 groups of **10** cupcakes = **50** cupcakes altogether

10 20 30 40 50 60 70 80 90 100

Groups of 10 — 101

Stripe has arranged these snacks in groups of 10. Circle each group, then write the numbers in the boxes at the bottom to finish the sentence.

6 groups of **10** snacks = **60** snacks altogether

10 20 30 40 50 60 70 80 90 100

Groups of 10 — 102

Bun's found some groups of 10 fish to catch in her net. Circle each group, then write the numbers in the boxes at the bottom to finish the sentence.

7 groups of **10** fish = **70** fish altogether

10 20 30 40 50 60 70 80 90 100

Groups of 10 — 103

Spike wants to catch these groups of 10 fish. Circle each group, then write the numbers in the boxes at the bottom to finish the sentence.

8 groups of **10** fish = **80** fish altogether

10 20 30 40 50 60 70 80 90 100

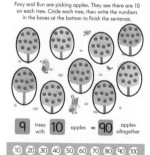

Groups of 10 — 104

Foxy and Bun are picking apples. They see there are 10 on each tree. Circle each tree, then write the numbers in the boxes at the bottom to finish the sentence.

9 trees with **10** apples = **90** apples altogether

10 20 30 40 50 60 70 80 90 100

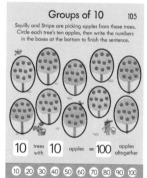

Groups of 10 — 105

Squilly and Stripe are picking apples from these trees. Circle each tree's ten apples, then write the numbers in the boxes at the bottom to finish the sentence.

10 trees with **10** apples = **100** apples altogether

10 20 30 40 50 60 70 80 90 100

Equal groups — 106

Describe these groups in two different ways. Write in the empty boxes how many groups there are, and how many birds there are altogether.

4 groups of **10** birds = **40** birds

4 x 10 = **40** birds

Equal groups — 107

Describe these groups in two different ways. Write in the empty boxes how many groups there are, and how many butterflies there are altogether.

5 groups of **10** butterflies = **50** butterflies

5 x 10 = **50** butterflies

Equal groups — 108

Describe these groups in two different ways. Write in the empty boxes how many groups there are, and how many flowers there are altogether.

3 groups of **10** flowers = **30** flowers

3 x 10 = **30** flowers

Answers

Equal groups 109

Describe these groups in two different ways.
Write in the empty boxes how many groups there
are, and how many worms there are altogether.

2 groups of 10 worms = 20 worms

2 x 10 = 20 worms

Equal groups 110

Describe this group in two different ways.
Write in the empty boxes how many groups there
are, and how many bugs there are altogether.

1 group of 10 bugs = 10 bugs

1 x 10 = 10 bugs

Equal groups 111

Describe these groups in two different ways.
Write in the empty boxes how many groups there
are, and how many acorns there are altogether.

7 groups of 10 acorns = 70 acorns

7 x 10 = 70 acorns

Equal groups 112

Describe these groups in two different ways.
Write in the empty boxes how many groups there
are, and how many leaves there are altogether.

6 groups of 10 leaves = 60 leaves

6 x 10 = 60 leaves

Equal groups 113

Describe these groups in two different ways.
Write in the empty boxes how many groups there
are, and how many stars there are altogether.

9 groups of 10 stars = 90 stars

9 x 10 = 90 stars

Equal groups 114

Describe these groups in two different ways.
Write in the empty boxes how many groups there
are, and how many pencils there are altogether.

8 groups of 10 pencils = 80 pencils

8 x 10 = 80 pencils

Equal groups 115

Describe these groups in two different ways.
Write in the empty boxes how many groups there
are, and how many balls there are altogether.

10 groups of 10 balls = 100 balls

10 x 10 = 100 balls

Calculation pairs 116

Stripe and Squilly have been picking peaches. Fill in
the numbers in the calculations below to see how many
peaches they each have, and to see if Squilly is right.

I think we both have
the same number of
peaches, Stripe!

Stripe's
calculation: 10 x 4 = 40

Squilly's
calculation: 4 x 10 = 40

Calculation pairs 117

Fill in the blanks to complete two different calculations
for each group of balls. One has been done for you.

10 x 5 = 50
5 x 10 = 50

10 x 3 = 30
3 x 10 = 30

10 x 4 = 40
4 x 10 = 40

Answers

Calculation pairs 118

Fill in the blanks to complete two different calculations for each group of marbles. One has been done for you.

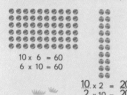

10 x 6 = 60
6 x 10 = 60

10 x 2 = 20
2 x 10 = 20

10 x 1 = 10
1 x 10 = 10

10 times table 119

Trace over the dotted numbers and fill in the empty boxes to finish these calculations in the 10 times table.

1 x 10 = 10   6 x 10 = 60

2 x 10 = 20   7 x 10 = 70

3 x 10 = 30   8 x 10 = 80

4 x 10 = 40   9 x 10 = 90

5 x 10 = 50   10 x 10 = 100

10 times table 120

Trace over the dotted numbers and fill in the empty boxes to finish these calculations in the 10 times table.

10 x 1 = 10   10 x 6 = 60

10 x 2 = 20   10 x 7 = 70

10 x 3 = 30   10 x 8 = 80

10 x 4 = 40   10 x 9 = 90

10 x 5 = 50   10 x 10 = 100

Calculation match-up 121

Help Coco finish these calculations. Draw a line to match each one to its answer. One has been done for you.

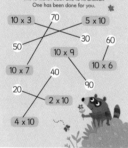

10 x 3   70   5 x 10
50   30   60
         10 x 9
10 x 7   40   10 x 6
20   90
        2 x 10
4 x 10

How many tens? 122

Finish these shell calculations. To help, you could draw around groups of 10 shells until they are all in groups, then count the groups.

2 x 10 = 20

6 x 10 = 60

How many tens? 123

Complete these butterfly calculations. To help, you could draw around groups of 10 butterflies until they are all in groups, then count the groups.

7 x 10 = 70

5 x 10 = 50

How many tens? 124

Finish these bee calculations. To help, you could draw around groups of 10 bees until they are all in groups, then count the groups.

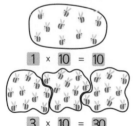

1 x 10 = 10

3 x 10 = 30

How many tens? 125

Complete these star calculations. To help, you could draw around groups of 10 stars until they are all in groups, then count the groups.

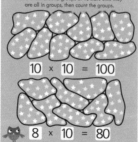

10 x 10 = 100

8 x 10 = 80

How many tens? 126

Finish these acorn calculations. To help, you could draw around groups of 10 acorns until they are all in groups, then count the groups.

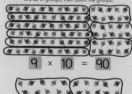

9 x 10 = 90

4 x 10 = 40